Enid Blyton's

MAGICAL TALES

The Naughty Little Squirrel

and other stories

To Michela

Christmas 2000

Love from

G'ma & G'Ded.

D0961567

This is a Parragon Book

© Parragon 1997

13-17 Avonbridge Trading Estate,
Atlantic Road, Avonmouth, Bristol
Produced by The Templar Company plc,
Pippbrook Mill, London Road, Dorking,
Surrey RH4 1JE

Text copyright © Enid Blyton Ltd 1926-29

These stories were first published in Sunny Stories,
Teacher's Treasury, Two Years in the Infant School,
Read to Us, New Friends and Old and
The Daily Mail Annual.

Enid Blyton's signature mark is a registered
trademark of Enid Blyton Limited.

Edited by Caroline Repchuk and Dugald Steer

Designed by Mark Kingsley-Monks

Printed and bound in Italy

ISBN 0 7525 1709 0 (Hardback)
ISBN 0 7525 2319 8 (Paperback)

Enid Blyton's

The Naughty Little Squirrel

and other stories

PARRAGON

Contents

The Naughty Little Squirrel

ONCE upon a time there were two red squirrels. They were pretty creatures, with soft fur, big bushy tails, and lovely bright eyes. They lived together in the trees and had a big nest made of twigs, bark, moss and leaves. They had built it very strongly, and it was cosy and warm inside.

In the nest were four baby squirrels. They were just like their mother and father, but were not so big. They had not been much out of the nest, but each day the mother squirrel took them for a little scamper up and down the trees and then led them safely back to their nest.

One little squirrel was most adventurous. He wanted to go farther than his mother wished to take him.

"No, Bushy," she said to him. "You must not go any farther. You might meet a red fox on the ground – or a big kestrel might see you and pounce on you. Keep with me."

Frisky, Bobs and Tufty, the other little squirrels, were good and obedient. They did exactly as they were told. But Bushy really was naughty!

"If Mother won't let me go where I want to, I shall wait until we are left alone in the nest and then I shall jump out and go adventuring by myself!" he told the others.

"Don't be naughty, Bushy!" said Tufty.

"I shall be just as naughty as I feel like!" said Bushy. Wasn't he a rascal?

Now, the very next day the mother and father squirrel went to talk to some other squirrels in the trees at the other side of the wood. They leapt from bough to bough, as light as feathers, and were out of sight in a moment. Bushy poked his little red head out of the nest.

"I'm off for an adventure!" he told his brothers and sisters – and off he went! Down the tree he scampered and hunted about on the ground for a special toadstool his mother had told him about. He couldn't find one, so he scampered between the trees to see if he could find anything else nice to eat.

Suddenly he saw a big red creature watching him from under a bush. There was a large hole there, and the red animal had come silently out of this hole.

The little squirrel looked at the big animal. It was a fox but he

did not know it. He thought that
the fox must be some sort of
strange squirrel. So he spoke to
him boldly.

"Good morning!"

"Good morning!" said the fox,
his eyes gleaming as he watched
the fat little squirrel bounding
about. "Would you like to pay a
visit to my home?"

"Where do you live?" asked
the squirrel.

"I live under the ground," said
the fox.

"What a strange place to live!"
said the little squirrel in surprise.
"My home is up in the trees!"

"My home is very cosy," said

the fox. "Do come to dinner with me, squirrel. You look hungry."

"I am hungry!" said Bushy, feeling rather excited to think that such a big creature should be so nice and polite to him. "I will come with you."

"You go first!" said the fox, and he waved his paw to his hole. Bushy scampered over to pop down it – but suddenly he heard a little barking noise overhead, from the trees. He looked up. It was his mother, peeping down at him in fright.

"Bushy! Bushy! That's a fox! He will eat you for his dinner! Run quickly!"

The fox gave a snarl of anger and ran at Bushy. But the frightened little squirrel whisked round and scampered off. The fox raced after him.

"Run up the tree trunk as I have taught you to!" called his mother. Bushy scampered up – but the fox snapped at his tail and took two or three hairs out of the tip! What a narrow escape for poor Bushy!

His mother took him back to the nest.

"You see what happens to naughty, disobedient squirrels," she scolded. "If I had not come by just then you would have gone down the fox's hole and been eaten. You may think you are a clever, adventurous squirrel, but you are not. You are very stupid. Wait till you know more of the world before you run off alone like that!"

Poor Bushy! He settled down at the bottom of the nest and didn't say a word. He was frightened and ashamed. His tail hurt. He had very nearly lost it!

"I won't go out by myself until my mother says I may!" he thought. And after that he was just as good and obedient as the others. He did have a narrow escape, didn't he?

Mr Wumble s Treasure

ONCE upon a time there was an old man who found a treasure in his garden. It was a little tin full of gold pieces. There were twenty of them, and Mr Wumble was full of joy to think that he had found such a wonderful treasure.

He took the gold pieces to his wife and she exclaimed in the greatest delight:

"Now we are rich! We are very rich! Oh, Mr Wumble, what a wonderful find!"

"I must go out straightaway and tell my friends all about it," said Mr Wumble. So he put on his best hat and coat, brushed his boots and set out.

All his friends were at market that day so Mr Wumble went there. He soon met Mr Timble and Mr Ho-Ho, and he stopped them and told them of his marvellous find.

"Yes," he said, "I was digging in the garden, and I found a tin full of gold! What do you think of that?"

"How much gold was there?" asked Mr Ho-Ho.

"Oh, quite fifty pieces," said Mr Wumble, thinking that twenty didn't sound very many. "Quite fifty, and maybe more."

Soon he met Mr and Mrs

Waitabit, and he told them his story too.

"Yes," he said, "I was digging in the garden, and I found a tin full of gold. What do you think of that?"

"How much gold was there?"

"Oh, quite a hundred pieces," said Mr Wumble, thinking that he might as well say a hundred as fifty. "Quite a hundred and maybe more."

Then up came Mr Too-Thin and his good friend Mr Tubby. Mr Wumble hurried to tell them his story.

"Yes," he said. "I was digging in the garden and I found a tin full of gold. What do you think of that?"

"How much gold was there?"

"Oh, quite five hundred pieces," said Mr Wumble, anxious to make everyone more surprised than ever. "Quite five hundred and maybe more."

"My!" said Mr Tubby. "That's a fortune! What have you done with it?"

"Oh, I left it on the dresser," said Mr Wumble.

"Left it on the dresser!" cried everyone. "Why! It might easily be stolen!"

"You should buy a safe!" said Mr Tubby. "That's what you

should do. See, there is a man
over there who has a fine safe,
which would hold your money
well. Come and buy it. You have
plenty of money, and it is your
duty to spend a little to keep the
rest in safety."

Everyone went with Mr
Wumble to the man with the
safe. It was a lovely safe, there
was no doubt about it. It was
very heavy and had six different
keys. Mr Wumble felt that he
would be proud to have it.

"I will come home with you
and carry the safe on my
shoulders," said the man. "It is
very heavy. You can pay me

when we get home."

"You ought to have a big book to write down how you spend all your fortune," said Mrs Waitabit. "If you don't do that, everyone will cheat you, and you will never know where your money goes. You had better buy a big book."

"Yes," said everyone. "You must buy a big book to put down how you spend your money."

Then Mr Wumble was taken to another man who was selling books in which to write down any money that was spent. There was one book he had which was very grand. It had gold edges, and was stamped with little gold dots all over the cover. It had a little lock on the front with a key, and Mr Wumble thought it was very fine indeed.

"If you have a fortune, you had better buy this book," said the man. "You don't want a common little notebook. You want a book fit for a rich man."

"I will have that fine book then," said Mr Wumble, feeling very grand.

"Very well," said the man. "I will carry it to your house for you, and you can pay me when we get there."

"Have you a good pen to write down all your bills?" asked Mr

Ho-Ho. "You ought to buy a fine pen, you know."

"There is a man here who sells all kinds of the most wonderful pens," said Mr Waitabit. "Come and see him."

So Mr Wumble was taken to the man who sold pens. When he heard all about Mr Wumble's fortune, he took a little golden box from his pocket and opened it. Inside lay a beautiful green pen with strange words written up and down the holder.

"Are you good at sums?" asked the man.

"Not very," said Mr Wumble, who couldn't even add seven and

eight together without making a mistake in the sum.

"Can you write well?" asked the man.

"Not very," said Mr Wumble, and he blushed red because his spelling was really dreadful.

"Ah!" said the man, "then this is exactly the pen you want. It has some special magic in it, and as soon as you take it into your hands and rest the point on your book it will add up all your sums without making a single mistake, and will write from morning to night and never get a word wrong. You should buy this pen Mr Wumble. You will never regret it, for it will save you many a hard day's work."

"I will have it," said Mr Wumble, thinking what a marvellous pen it was.

"I will take it home for you," said the man, "and you can pay me when you get there."

Then the man with the safe, the man with the book and the man with the pen and Mr Wumble all turned homewards. When they got there Mr Wumble smelt a very nice smell indeed, and he guessed his wife was cooking a turkey for him.

"Wife," he said. "See what I have bought. Here is a safe to

keep our money in, a book to write down how we spend it, and a pen to write with. The pen will add up all our sums without a mistake."

"Oh my!" said the wife, and she ran to see these wonderful things. The man with the safe rested his heavy burden on the floor and asked for his money.

"Ten pounds," he said. So Mr Wumble paid him ten gold pieces and he went off quite happily. Then the man with the book put it down on the table and asked for his money.

"Three pounds, please," he said. So Mr Wumble paid him

three gold pieces and he went off whistling.

Then the man with the wonderful pen put it down on the mantelpiece and asked for his money.

"Six pounds, please," he said. So Mr Wumble paid him six pieces of gold and he went off singing like a blackbird.

"Now," said Mr Wumble, feeling very important. "I will write down all we have spent in this book with this magic pen."

He took up his pen and it began to write. It certainly was wonderful. It did the sum in a flash – and then Mr Wumble began to look rather blue.

"Oh my, oh my!" he said. "The pen has done the sum, and the book says we have only got one gold piece left. See if the book is right, wife."

But when Mrs Wumble looked into the tin it was empty. Not a single gold piece was there!

"Oh!" she said. "Of course, I spent one gold piece on the turkey – so there's no treasure left at all, Mr Wumble!"

"And I've bought a safe to keep it in, a book to put down how we spend it, and a pen to do the sums for us!" cried Mr Wumble in dismay. "Why, there's no treasure at all left to put in the safe!"

"Oh, you foolish, stupid man!" cried his wife, in a temper, and she took up her rolling-pin and bashed him on the shoulders with it. Then they began to quarrel and fight, and they didn't stop till the safe lay broken on the floor, the book had all its pages torn, and the pen was smashed to a hundred pieces. Then the silly couple stopped and looked at one another. Mrs Wumble began to cry.

"Oh, what a pair of sillies we are!" she wept. "We have spoilt everything."

"Never mind," said Mr Wumble. "It's all my fault. If I hadn't told everyone that I had found a much bigger fortune than I really did, this would never have happened. Nobody would have made me buy all those things if they had known it was only twenty gold pieces I had found."

"Well," said Mrs Wumble, drying her eyes. "Let's sit down and eat the turkey. That's the only bit of treasure that's left."

But alas! The turkey was all burnt up in the oven, for they had quite forgotten about it in their quarrel. So they sadly threw

34

it into the dustbin and sat down to a dinner of bread and cheese.

"We won't be so foolish the next time I find a treasure," said Mr Wumble.

But he never did find one again. Wasn't it a pity?

The Vanishing
Potatoes

TIMES were very bad in the Village of Tuppence. All the brownies went hungry, and they grew thin and pale. Bron, their chief, shared all his apples and pears, and potatoes with the others, but when they were gone the brownies really didn't know where to turn for a meal.

Only one brownie was well off – and that was Leery, the old, ugly brownie who lived by himself in a tiny cottage just outside the village. He had thousands of potatoes, and was never hungry, for he could always bake two or three for himself whenever he wanted to.

"Ho!" he often thought to himself. "Bron may be king, but I am better off than he is! I shan't share my potatoes with anyone, not I! Perhaps the brownies will make me their chief when they see how rich I am. I never thought Bron was a good king. He was always too kind – look at him now, no richer than all the other brownies, because he has given away all his apples, pears and potatoes!"

Now Leery kept his potatoes in a shed outside, and one day he saw a small brownie peeping through a crack at the piles of potatoes. He chased him off angrily, and then became afraid for his store.

"Suppose someone comes and steals my potatoes!" he thought. "That would never do! I don't trust these brownies. I think I shall bring all my potatoes into my cottage – then they will be under my eye and no one can steal any!"

So the next morning the mean little brownie filled his barrow full of potatoes and wheeled them into his small kitchen. He tipped them out on the floor and then went back for another barrow load. He spent all morning doing this and, by the time it was midday, the shed was empty – and his kitchen was piled high with brown potatoes!

"Goodness!" said Leery, scratching his head as he looked round at the hundreds of potatoes. "There's not much room for anything now. I'd better take my chairs into the bedroom – and the table too."

So he carried all the chairs and the table into the bedroom. He only left himself a small stool to sit on by the fire. There he sat, looking at all his lovely potatoes, pleased to think that he had so many more than anyone else.

Now, when the brownies saw

Leery wheeling his potatoes from the shed to his kitchen they were very cross.

"I suppose he is afraid we might go and take some!" grumbled Bron. "It would serve him right if we did! Mean old thing, never offering anyone even a bad potato! He can't possibly eat all those himself. He ought to share them with us."

"Well, Bron, shall we go and ask him to share them?" said another Brownie. "He might, you know."

"I'll go!" said Bron. And so off he went.

He knocked at Leery's door

and Leery called: "Come in!"

Bron stepped inside – and how he stared to see all the floor covered and piled with brown potatoes, and Leery hunched up on a small stool!

"Good morning, Leery," he said. "I've come to ask you if you will share your hoard of potatoes with the village. You have too many to eat by yourself, and the others are very hungry."

"What are you thinking of?" cried Leery, in a temper. "Give my potatoes away? After spending so much time and trouble in growing them! Not I! You're a poor sort of king, Bron, it seems to me, to let the Village of Tuppence get into such a state – and, by the way, I think it was very foolish of you to share out all your food with the others. What's the good of being king unless you are much richer than anyone else?"

"What's the good of being king unless you can help your people when they are in trouble?" said Bron indignantly. "My people love me, and I am pleased to help them. I suppose you think you'd make a much better king yourself!"

"Well, of course I do," said Leery. "Look at all my potatoes!

I've hundreds more than anyone! I am rich enough to be king twice over! And I'm quite sure all the brownies would much rather have me as their head than you!"

"I'm quite sure they wouldn't!" said Bron. "And I do think it's horrid of you, Leery, to wheel all your potatoes out of your shed, as if you were afraid somebody would steal them."

"Well, nobody can take them now," said Leery. "I'd like to see a brownie steal any from me! Ho, ho! Nobody could. Anyone can come and try – but they're under my eye now, and not a potato can go out of this room without my seeing it!"

Bron was disgusted with Leery. He went out of the cottage and banged the door. He told the other brownies all that Leery had said, and they were very angry.

"Oh, so he said that anybody could go and try to take his potatoes, did he!" said Skippetty, a sharp-eyed brownie, thoughtfully. "Well, let's all go, one by one, and take his potatoes! We'll play a nice little trick on the mean old thing!"

"How?" cried the brownies, crowding round the small Skippetty.

"Listen," said Skippetty. "We'll

pretend that we are thinking of making him our king – and we will all go to his cottage, one after another, and talk to him about it. I will paint each of you at the back with strong glue – and, as there is nowhere at all to sit down except on piles of potatoes, we will each sit down on them – and when we get up there will be a dozen potatoes sticking to us!"

"Yes, but Leery will be sure to see them when we turn to go out," said Bron.

"Oh no, he won't!" said Skippetty, grinning. "You have to walk out backwards when you go

out from a king's presence, you
know – so we will each walk out
backwards, and Leery won't see
a single potato! He will be so
pleased to think that we are
being polite to him! Now,
where's my pot of glue?"

In a few minutes twelve
brownies were all painted at the
back with strong glue. How they
giggled and laughed! Skippetty
said he would be the first one to
go to visit Leery, and he set off
right away. He knocked at the
door – blim-blam!

"Come in!" shouted Leery.
Skippetty went in – and how he
stared at all those potatoes!

"Good morning, Leery," he began politely. "I've come to say that I've heard from Bron that you would like to be king."

Leery beamed broadly all over his ugly face.

"Yes," he said. "I'm richer than anybody now, you know."

"Do you mind if I sit down and talk about it?" asked Skippetty politely.

"Not at all," said Leery, waving his hand towards a pile of potatoes. "I've taken all the chairs into the bedroom. Sit down on the potatoes. It won't hurt them."

Skippetty sat down hard,

hoping that some very big potatoes would stick to him. Then he began to talk to Leery, and flattered the silly brownie so much that Leery nearly fell off his stool in delight.

"Well, Leery, I really must go now," said Skippetty at last, getting up from the potatoes he had been sitting on. "Goodbye. As you are now so grand, and may be crowned king any day, I will walk out backwards from your presence to show you how much I respect you!"

Leery could hardly believe his ears! To think that cheeky little Skippetty should be so civil to him! It was wonderful!

"Yes, do walk out backwards," he said grandly. "I am glad to see you know your manners when you talk to a king."

So Skippetty solemnly stood up, and then began to walk carefully backwards to the door. He opened it, grinned wickedly and went out, still backwards. He slammed the door and went down the path. Just round the next corner all the other brownies were waiting for him – and how they laughed when they saw him! He turned himself round – and they stared in delight at fourteen large potatoes sticking fast to his back and legs!

"Oooh, Skippetty, what a lovely lot of potatoes!" said the brownies, and they pulled them off to eat for their dinner. How they chuckled when they heard all that Skippetty had said to stupid, greedy old Leery!

That afternoon two more brownies, one after another, went to call on Leery. They spoke solemnly to him about being king, and he was more and more delighted. They sat on the piles of potatoes, feeling them sticking to them, and could hardly keep from giggling.

One brownie brought away

twelve with him and the other, who was a bigger fellow, took away sixteen! All the brownies shouted with laughter when the two brownies told them how delighted Leery was when they walked backwards most politely as they left him. They though that was really a great joke.

"He deserves to be tricked," said Skippetty, "He is the meanest fellow that ever lived!"

Leery was so pleased and proud to find the brownies really seemed to be thinking of making him king, that at first he didn't notice his potatoes were going. But, after six brownies had visited him and talked to him, he suddenly thought that his potato piles seemed to be growing smaller and smaller.

"Strange!" said Leery, rubbing his chin in astonishment. "How is that, now? Surely those brownies are not taking potatoes away with them? I shall watch very carefully when the next one comes, and see that he does not put any in his pockets."

So when the next brownie came to call on Leery he watched him very carefully. But he did not see one potato being taken, for the brownie kept his hands in front of him all the time

and did not once put them into
his pocket.

Yet when that little brownie
had walked politely backwards
out of the room there seemed
less potatoes than ever. It really
was very strange indeed.

Leery began to get worried. He
looked hard at the next brownie
all the time he was talking – but,
no, he could not see him even
touch a potato with his hands! It
was very peculiar.

Then Leery thought he would
call a meeting of the brownies
and tell them to make him king
at once. Then he could set them
all to watch for the thief,

whoever he was, and stop him from stealing his potatoes. He could not think where they were going to!

So he sent a message to them by the next brownie that called – and how everybody grinned.

"We'll all go," said Bron, who was enjoying the joke as much as anyone. "We'll all be painted with glue – and what a lot of potatoes Leery will miss when we've gone!"

So off they all went, and filed in at Leery's door. They sat down hard on the potatoes, and listened as Leery explained they should make him king at once.

"If we make you king, will you be kind and share your potatoes with us, just as Bron did?" asked Skippetty, his little dark eyes twinkling.

That was too much for Leery. "Certainly not!" he said angrily. "I'm not so foolish. I might give you one each, perhaps. Anyway, none of you look hungry or thin now – you have all got quite nice and fat again, I can't think why!"

"Well, I'm sorry, Leery," said Skippetty, getting up, "but I'm afraid we can't make you king just yet. You may have plenty of potatoes, but you've got very little else. A king wants a kind heart as well as piles of potatoes. Goodbye!"

He went out backwards, and so did all the others. Leery stared at them in rage. When the last one had gone he looked at his potatoes in a panic! There were hardly any left at all! Wherever in the wide world had they gone?

He rushed to the door to call back the brownies and tell them about the strange disappearance. He saw them all walking down the street, chattering and laughing merrily – and he looked at them in surprise. Whatever was the matter with their backs? They seemed to be covered with knobbly brown things!

And then Leery saw what the knobbly things were – potatoes, of course! In a flash he saw the trick that had been played on him, and he tore after the brownies in a terrible temper, shaking his fists and stamping his feet in rage.

"You wicked robbers!" he cried. "You mean, horrid things! You've stolen my potatoes, yes you have! I'll put you in prison!"

"You can't!" laughed the brownies. "Bron is our king – and he wouldn't put us in prison, we are sure! Remember, Leery, you told him that anyone might

take your potatoes if he could –
and so we have! We have only
obeyed you, that's all! If you
hadn't been so vain, thinking you
were going to be king, you would
have seen what we were doing!"

"Give me back my potatoes!"
yelled Leery.

"We've eaten most of them,"
grinned Skippetty. "Don't worry,
Leery – when better times come
we will pay you for the ones we
have taken. It serves you right to
be tricked – you are too mean for
anything!"

Back went Leery to his cottage,
crying tears of rage all down his
long nose – and would you

believe it, when he got to his door there was not a single potato left in the kitchen! The rats had popped in and taken every last one whilst he had gone after the brownies!

So Leery had to go hungry too, and it did him a lot of good. He felt far too ashamed to face the brownies of Tuppence Village, so he packed and left. He turned over a new leaf and tried not to be mean – and I shouldn't be surprised to hear that he becomes a king one day. But I'm quite sure he won't let anyone walk out backwards when they take leave of him. Aren't you?

Cosy s Good Turn

BUNDLE came running into the garden to find Cosy. He had an old and rather smelly kipper in his mouth.

He dropped it and barked for Cosy. "Cosy! Cosy! Now where can that cat be? What on earth's the good of finding this nice old kipper for her, out of Mrs Brown's dustbin, if she doesn't come when she's called?"

Cosy sat on top of the wall, washing her face with her paws. She had heard Bundle barking, but she didn't hurry down to see what he wanted.

"I expect he wants to play 'Chase-my-Tail' or 'Roll-Over-

and-Over,'" thought Cosy. "What silly games he knows!"

"Woof, woof!" barked Bundle, and then a faint smell of kipper came to Cosy's nose. She sniffed. Then she leapt straight down from the wall and ran to Bundle, her tail up in the air behind her.

"I thought you were never coming," said Bundle. "I've done you a good turn, Cosy. I've found you an old kipper. It's been eaten a bit, but it smells fine. I was just going to eat it myself if you didn't come at once!"

Cosy purred, and rubbed herself against Bundle's silky coat. "You're kind to do me a good turn," she said.

"Well," said Bundle, watching Cosy eat the kipper, "you know what Mistress always says, don't you? She says, 'One good turn deserves another!'"

"Does she really?" said Cosy. "Well, you do me another good turn then, Bundle. I don't mind."

"Don't be silly. It doesn't mean that I do you another good turn," said Bundle. "It means that you do me one – in return for mine, you see."

"Oh," said Cosy, crunching up the last of the kipper. "All right. I'll do you a good turn, too. The very next thing you want, tell me and I'll get it for you."

"Thanks very much," said Bundle, pleased.

"I'll let you know when I want something. You do smell nice, Cosy. You smell of kipper now, not cat. Come and lie down beside me so that I can keep on sniffing you."

Now, the very next day was hot, so hot that Bundle lay and panted with his tongue out. Someone had spilt his water and there was none to drink. There were no puddles anywhere. It was too far to go to the stream. But oh, how thirsty he was!

"You look silly with your

tongue out like that," said Cosy. "Do put it back."

"It comes out as soon as I put it in," said Bundle. "It always does that when I'm hot. Oh, how thirsty I am! Is there any milk about, Cosy? There's no water."

"I've drunk all mine," said Cosy. "I'll go and see if there's any milk in the larder, Bundle. If there is, I know how to knock the jug over and spill the milk on the floor. Then you can come and lick it up."

But the larder door was shut. It always was when Cosy was anywhere about. She went back to Bundle and lay down.

"The larder door's shut," she said. "You'll just have to be thirsty, Bundle."

"Well, why can't you do me that good turn you promised me?" said Bundle. "I'm very thirsty, and you ought to do something about it. You do me my good turn now. Get me some milk to drink!"

"If I knew where the milk came from I'd go and get some for you," said Cosy. "Where does the milkman get his milk from?"

"From a cow, silly," said Bundle. "All our milk comes from cows."

"Does it really?" said Cosy in

surprise. "Well, I never knew that before! How kind of the cows! I know, Bundle – I'll take a jug and go and ask that big red-and-white cow in the field for some milk for you. That would be an awfully good turn, wouldn't it?"

"Yes," said Bundle, panting. "Hurry up then or I shall die of thirst!"

Cosy got a little jug. Then she set off to the fields. Daisy, the big red-and-white cow, was lying down in a cool corner, chewing.

"Cows are always chewing," thought Cosy. "They never seem to stop. Hello, Daisy! Do you think I could possibly have some milk, please?"

"Well," said Daisy, still chewing, "one good turn deserves another, you know. There's some lovely, dark green grass in the next field, all long and juicy, but I can't reach it over the hedge myself. You go and get me a bit of that and I'll fill your jug for you."

"All right," said Cosy, and she ran to the hedge. She squeezed through it and looked about for the grass. She soon saw it growing by a moist ditch, long and juicy. Clopper the horse was standing near it, munching.

Cosy ran to get the grass. She began pulling it up. Clopper stopped munching and stared straight at her.

"Hey!" he said. "That's my grass. It's the best grass in the whole field."

"Oh," said Cosy. "Well, I want some for Daisy the cow, then she'll give me some milk. Can't I take some?"

"Now look here, one good turn deserves another," said Clopper. "You can have some of my grass if you'll do something for me."

"I seem to be doing no end of good turns," said Cosy.

"Well, I'm longing for a nice

green apple," said Clopper. "See that cottage over there? Well, in the back garden there's an apple tree, and it's got fine green apples on it. You get me one of those and I'll let you take some of that grass."

"All right," said Cosy, and she ran over the field towards the cottage. She jumped up on the wall round it and then down into the garden. Then in a trice she was up the apple tree.

She bumped her head hard against the biggest green apple she could see. It fell to the ground with a bump. Cosy was just about to run down the tree when she heard a cross voice:

"What are you doing up there, knocking down my apples!"

Down below was a plump little woman, trying to mend a clothes line so that she could hang out her washing. She was looking up at Cosy, surprised and cross.

"Well, you see, I wanted to get an apple for Clopper," said Cosy. "Could I have the one I knocked down?"

"Well, one good turn deserves another," said the plump little woman. "If you'll go and borrow Mrs Miggle's rope for me, then I'll give you the apple. My clothes line is broken and I must have another!"

"Another good turn!" sighed Cosy, and ran down the lane to the next cottage, where Mrs Miggle was sitting in the sun, shelling peas.

"May I borrow your rope, please?" asked Cosy. "You see, if I take it to your next-door neighbour, she will give me an apple for Clopper, and he will give me his best grass for Daisy, and she will give me milk for Bundle. I am trying to do him a good turn."

"So you want my rope!" said Mrs Miggle. "Well, what I always say is – one good turn deserves another. If I lend you my rope, you must do something for me. You run down to the old man who lives at the corner, and ask him to let me have just a few more peas. I haven't enough. Take this basket with you."

"I keep on and on doing good turns!" said Cosy, but she ran off with the basket in her mouth. She soon came to the cottage at the corner. The old man was indoors, looking into his larder. He seemed rather cross.

"Please," said Cosy, "may I have a few peas? Mrs Miggle hasn't enough."

"I'll go and pick them," said

the old man. "I like to do people a good turn. But one good turn deserves another, you know, little cat. You can do me a good turn, whilst I pick the peas."

"I thought you were going to say that," said poor Cosy.

"Now just have a look in this larder of mine!" said the old man. "Mice have been in it again. One ran away just as I opened the door. You catch me those mice by the time I come back and I'll give you the peas!"

He went out and Cosy sat down quietly behind the door. She could smell plenty of mice, no doubt about that.

"Well, anyway at least I shall be doing myself a good turn now, as well as the old man," she thought. "Because I rather like catching mice!"

Soon Cosy had caught three mice. The old man came with the basket half full of peas. He was delighted to see what Cosy had done for him.

"You have done me a good turn," he said. "And you've done my cat a good turn too – she's too old to catch mice now. Here are the peas. Remember what I said? 'One good turn deserves another!'"

"Goodbye!" said Cosy, and she

left the cottage, taking the peas with her.

She went to Mrs Miggle's and put the basket down. "Here are the peas," she said. "Now may I borrow the rope?"

"Here it is," said Mrs Miggle, and gave it to her. "Thank you. You see what I meant when I said, 'One good turn de...'"

But Cosy didn't even stop to listen. She tore off to the plump little woman next door, trailing the rope out behind her like a long snake.

"Well, I thought you were never coming!" said the little woman, quite crossly. "I've been waiting such a time. Now, take your apple and go. And always remember, 'One good...'"

"I know it by heart, thank you," said Cosy quite rudely, and then she ran off with the apple. She came to Clopper and rolled it at his feet.

"What a time you've been," said Clopper. "I had quite given you up. I suppose you've been chattering away to someone. Take what grass you want – and remember, 'One...'"

"I don't want to remember it," said Cosy, dragging up the grass crossly. "I've been doing nothing but good turns for ages and ages.

You may have done me one good turn, but I tell you I've done heaps! I can't seem to stop doing them. I ..."

"What a lot you've got to say," said Clopper. "Ah – now you've got your mouth full of grass and you won't be able talk. Good. Now remember, 'One...'"

But Cosy had fled through he hedge and was on her way to the shady corner in the field where Daisy the cow still lay, chewing away. The little empty jug lay beside her.

"Here's your grass," said Cosy, and dropped it right down beside Daisy.

"I don't really know if I want it now," said Daisy. "You've been so long."

"Well!" said Cosy. "Of all the ungrateful, unkind..."

"All right, all right," said the cow hurriedly. "I'll have it. Don't lose your temper. You should always do a good turn cheerfully and quickly."

"Don't talk to me about good turns," said Cosy. "Just you do yours, Diasy, and give me some milk for poor old thirsty Bundle. He must have died of thirst by now, I've been so busy doing good turns for everybody!"

Daisy filled the jug with creamy milk. It looked simply lovely. "Now don't spill it," she said. "And remember..."

But Cosy wasn't going to remember anything but the milk. Thank goodness she had got it at last! She went carefully across the field, through the hedge, and into the garden. She looked about for Bundle. Ah, there he was, in the corner where it was cool. How pleased he would be to see the milk! Cosy trotted over and put the jug down carefully beside him.

"There you are, Bundle!" she said. "Lovely milk for you."

Bundle looked down his nose at it. "What, milk again?" he said. "I don't want any more. Mistress came out some time ago and filled your dish with rice pudding and milk. I ate it all up, and I can tell you the milk was very good! But I'm full up now and I don't want any more. It really makes me feel sick to look at all that milk."

"Well!" cried poor Cosy in a rage, and lost her temper altogether. She picked up the jug and threw it at Bundle. The milk spilt and went all over his silky coat. He was very angry.

"You horrid little cat!" Now look what you've done! There's milk all over my coat. And I thought you wanted to do me a good turn, not a bad one!"

"Well, I've tried," said Cosy, and tears trickled down her nose. "I've done ever so many good turns. I'm hot and tired and thirsty. I've been ever so far and got ever so many things for

people. And when I come back
with my good turn for you,
Bundle, you don't want it. I feel
very upset. And the milk's upset
too, and I do so badly want a
drink! You've had all my dinner,
too. Why did I ever try to do you
a good turn? It's all wasted!"

"You can always do me
another one some other time,"
said Bundle. But that wasn't the
right thing to say at all.

"What! Another good turn!"
cried Cosy. "No, no, Bundle –
you can do all the good turns in
future. Do you know, I went to
Daisy for some milk, and she
sent me to Clopper for some

special grass she wanted, and Clopper sent me to an apple tree for an apple, and the woman there sent me to Mrs Miggle's for a rope, and..."

"Goodness gracious!" said Bundle.

" ...And Mrs Miggle sent me to the old man at the corner for some more peas, and he told me to catch his mice!" wept poor Cosy. "And then I had to go back and take the peas to Mrs Miggle, and take the rope to the apple-woman, and take the apple to Clopper, and take the grass to Daisy, and bring the milk to you, and ..."

"And I'd had some, and you upset the milk in a temper," said Bundle. "Poor Cosy! What a shame! But now I'll do you a good turn, if you like! I'll sit quite still and let you lick all the milk that is dripping off my coat. Think what a nice meal that will be for you."

So Cosy sat and licked all the milk off Bundle's coat, and got a lots of hairs down her throat. Now she is sitting on the wall again, washing herself – and do you know what she is thinking?

"I wonder whether that was really a good turn that Bundle did me, letting me lick the milk off his coat?" she is saying to herself. "Or have I done *him* a good turn again? I've cleaned his coat for him, haven't I, and saved him from having a bath! Now, who did the good turn then?"

What do you think, children?

The Two
Clever
Brownies

"NOW," said Dame Bonnet, standing up on the platform, "now we have a grand competition!"

Everyone stopped talking to listen. It was a very merry evening at the village hall, and the brownies' band had been playing jolly tunes for everyone to dance to.

"A competition," said Hoppy. "I like competitions. I'd like to win one some day!"

"Sh!" said everyone, because Dame Bonnet had started speaking again.

She held up an orange and an apple. "It's the same competition that we have every year at this dance," she said. "Farmer Meadows is giving a whole crate of oranges and another whole crate of apples to the one who makes the nearest guess as to how many pips there are in this orange and apple!"

Everyone cheered. "Hurrah! Kind old Farmer Meadows!"

"It doesn't really matter who wins it," said Dame Bonnet, smiling round. "We know that the lucky one will share the fruit with us all!"

"Not if Mr Stingy wins it!" said Hoppy to Mr Lively, who was standing near him. "He won't share it with anyone. So let's hope he doesn't!"

Everybody went up and whispered their guesses into Dame Bonnet's ear and she wrote down the numbers they gave her. Hoppy guessed twenty orange-pips and twelve apple-pips. Mr Lively guessed just the opposite. Old Mother Winkles wanted to squeeze the orange a little in her hand to see if she could feel the pips, but she wasn't allowed to!

"And now," said Dame Bonnet, "I am going to cut open the orange and the apple, and ask Farmer Meadows to count them out for me!"

Dame Bonnet cut them open, and Farmer Meadows, who was very red-faced and burly, counted the pips very carefully indeed, one by one.

"Fifteen orange-pips and only eight apple-pips," he said. "Did anyone get the answer right?"

"I did! I did!" shouted Mr Stingy, in sudden delight. "I whispered those numbers in Dame Bonnet's ear. Didn't I, Dame Bonnet?"

"Yes, you did," said Dame Bonnet. "Well done, Mr Stingy. The crates of fruit are just at the back of the stage. I am sure you

would like to open them now,
and share your success with all
the others."

"Dear me, no!" said Mr Stingy
at once, looking quite horrified.
"They're mine. I won them fairly,
and I'm taking them home for
myself. They'll last me a nice
long time and save me buying
fruit. You can't make me open
them now!"

There was a shocked silence –
and then somebody hissed.
Somebody else booed. Soon the
hall was full of peculiar hissing
and booing noises.

"Boo and hiss all you like,"
said Mr Stingy. "You'll not get a

single orange or apple – no, not even a pip!"

And he took the two crates home right away, and never gave out a single orange or apple to anyone.

Ah, but wait, Mr Stingy! Hoppy and Mr Lively aren't going to let you do such a mean thing and get away with it. Oh, no! They are planning something – something that will make you very much annoyed tonight!

Now, about midnight that night, Mr Stingy woke up suddenly. Whatever was that noise in his garden? He sat up and listened.

"Woof-woof-woof! Woof-woof-woof! Ee-oo, ee-oo,eeeeee-oo, woof!"

"A dog! Whining and barking out there," said Mr Stingy, angrily. "Waking me up like this." He threw up his window and shouted loudly. "Now then! Go home, will you! Be quiet and go home!"

A loud growl came to his ears. "Urrrrrr-RRRRR!"

Mr Stingy was alarmed. Dear me – it sounded rather a large and fierce dog. He shut his window down a little way in case the dog might jump in.

"Woof-woof-woof!" barked the dog, and then whined dismally. "EEE-oo, eee-oo, EEEEE-oo!"

"Go away! How can I get to sleep with all that noise going on?" yelled Mr Stingy.

But the dog wouldn't go away. It woofed and howled and whined till it nearly drove Mr Stingy mad. It growled, too, so that he really was afraid of going out to chase it away.

He opened his window again and looked out. Where was the dog? He was sure it was hiding in the big bush by the front gate. He'd throw something at it and give it a fright. Then it would leap out and run away.

He looked round to see what to throw. Ah, yes – an orange! That would give the dog a good fright to be sure! He had plenty in the crate. He had opened both crates and had already eaten six oranges and apples. They were delicious.

He threw an orange into the bush. There was a yelp, and Mr Stingy grinned. Ha – that would send the brute away!

But it didn't. The woofing began again, even more loudly. It almost sounded as if there were two dogs now.

Mr Stingy threw another orange. Yelp, yelp! But no dog rushed out and away. Plonk! That was a third orange! Woof, woof, woof! Thud, that was another orange. Thud-thud-thud-thud-thud – off went another volley of oranges.

But that dog wouldn't budge from the bush. It yelped and growled, but it stayed there all the time.

Then Mr Stingy went quite mad. He hurled the rest of the oranges at the bush, and as he was a very good shot he hit it every single time he threw an orange at it.

"I can go out and pick them up tomorrow," he thought. "Dogs don't eat oranges. My word, there aren't any left now. I've thrown them all. All right, if that wretched dog begins to bark again, I'll start on the apples."

The dog was quiet for a minute or two, and Mr Stingy got thankfully into bed. But no sooner had he pulled the sheet up to his chin than the dog began all over again.

"Woof-woof-WOOF! WOOF!"

Mr Stingy shot out of bed in a furious rage. He began throwing the apples. Plonk-plonk-plonk! Three of them went into the bush at top speed.

"That'll teach you to disturb me!" he shouted, as loud yelps came from the bush, and out flew more apples. At last the crate of apples was empty and Mr Stingy yelled out of the window. "It won't be oranges or apples next, you bad dog – it will be something much worse!"

"Woooooooo!" said the dog, and then was silent.

Quite silent. Not a woof, not a whine, not a yelp.

Mr Stingy listened for a minute or two then crept into bed again. Would that barking begin once more? No – it didn't!

"I hope the dog is covered from head to tail with bruises from my apples and oranges!" thought Mr Stingy. "I'll go and pick them all up tomorrow. The oranges won't be damaged, but the apples may have a few dents in them. Well, it can't be helped. Anyway, they've stopped that dog barking!"

The next morning Mr Stingy went to collect his fruit – but, would you believe it, not one apple or orange was to be seen! They had completely disappeared.

Mr Stingy was most amazed. He crawled in and out and under

that bush for a whole hour, but not a single apple or orange did he find. He simply couldn't understand it.

Hoppy and Mr Lively came along and saw him crawling about. They nudged one another and laughed.

"What are you hunting for, Mr Stingy?" asked Hoppy, politely. "Worms?"

"No. My fruit," said Mr Stingy, snappily. "A dog came in the night and barked until I nearly went mad. So I threw my oranges and apples at him and stopped him. But now I can't find them."

"The dog must have eaten

them," said Hoppy, most solemnly, and Mr Lively gave a giggle. "Mr Lively, have we seen any dogs peeling oranges or eating apples this morning?"

"Not dogs," said Mr Lively, with another giggle. "Children – oh, yes, children, all over the village – munching away, bless their little hearts!"

Mr Stingy crawled out from the bush at once. "What do you mean? Not *my* apples and oranges, surely?"

"I never even saw your fruit, Mr Stingy," said Mr Lively. "You didn't offer anyone any, you know. So how am I to know if it's your oranges and apples the children are eating?"

"I don't understand this," said Mr Stingy, furiously, and he stood upright. "I threw them at that dog, and they went under this bush! Now, how could anyone know they were there, and take them for the children?"

"We're not much good at riddles," said Hoppy, grinning. "Though we might know the answer to that one, if we thought hard enough. Good morning to you, Mr Stingy. Try looking under another bush!"

They went off, laughing. Mr Stingy stared after them. Then

he suddenly heard a rather familiar noise, coming from down the street.

"Woof-woof-woof! Yelp-yelp! Ee-OOO! WOOF!"

"Oh! It was Hoppy and Lively pretending to be dogs under my bush last night! And I threw all my fruit at them – and they gathered it up and took it away to give to the children – which is what I ought to have done when I won the competition!" groaned Mr Stingy. "Now I haven't a single apple or orange left for myself! Wait till I get hold of Hoppy and Lively. Just wait!"

But he won't get hold of them –

they are much too clever for him! I wish I'd heard them howling under that bush, don't you? What a wonderful idea!

The Little Girl Who Didn't Think

ONCE upon a time there was
a little girl who didn't think.
Her name was Mollie, and her
mother was at her wit's end to
know how to make her think.
Her father was very upset about
it, too, but he couldn't do
anything either.

Mollie did all sorts of silly
things because she didn't think.
She nearly always put her shoes
on the wrong feet, and twice she
came down to breakfast in only
her petticoat because she had
forgotten to put her frock on.
And once she even went to
school on a Saturday, because
she had forgotten that the school

shut for the weekend. She was most astonished to find that no one was there.

Now, one day a new baby came to Mollie's house. He was the dearest, tiniest, loveliest thing, and he belonged to Mollie's mother and father.

Mollie loved him and loved him and loved him. She loved to hold him and sing to him. And the baby loved Mollie and smiled at her, and held her little finger in his funny little hand. Daddy was very pleased to see how fond Mollie was of the baby. He thought perhaps it would make her more careful in all sorts of ways. But it didn't seem to, for the very day after Daddy had thought that, Mollie was silly enough to shake out pepper in her porridge instead of sugar! And that meant her porridge was all wasted, of course.

The baby grew big and bonny – but then one day he fell ill. He lay in his crib and coughed and coughed, and the doctor came to see him every day.

"Will Baby get better?" Mollie kept asking. "Will Baby get better? Oh, please, please, make him better, Doctor!"

"He'll get better all right," said the doctor, smiling. "Don't you worry your little head! Help your Mummy all you possibly can by being a really good and thoughtful little girl."

But Mollie didn't help Mummy much. That very same evening she went to bed in all her clothes, because she had forgotten to get undressed. Did you ever hear such a dreadful thing?

One afternoon Mummy, Baby and Mollie were all together. Baby was lying on Mummy's lap fast asleep and she was very pleased.

"If only he doesn't have another bad coughing fit!" said Mummy. "But I don't think he will! Wake up, Mollie! You look as though you were half asleep! Go and fetch me the blue bottle you will see on the table downstairs in the dining-room. Then, if Baby does have a bad turn, I'll give him some of his new medicine."

Mollie didn't stir.

"Bless the child!" said Mummy. "Dreaming as usual! MOLLIE! Go and get me the blue bottle on the dining-room table!"

"The blue bottle on the dining-room table," said Mollie, dreamily. "Yes, Mummy."

She jumped up and went downstairs.

"Blue bottle," she said, "Blue bottle. I mustn't forget."

She went into the dining-room. On the table crawled a large bluebottle fly.

"Ah! There's the bluebottle!" said Mollie. "What a funny thing for Mummy to want. I must try to catch him."

But the bluebottle didn't want to be caught at all. With a loud buzz he flew off the table and banged straight into the window-pane. There he buzzed up and down angrily.

Mollie stood on a chair and tried to catch him. Off he flew again all round the room and came to rest on a picture. Buzz! Mollie just missed him again and he flew off.

Round and round the room they went, Mollie trying her very hardest to catch the bluebottle, but she couldn't, he was far too quick.

Upstairs, Mummy was wondering what in the world Mollie was doing.

And suddenly Baby woke up and began to cough badly.

"Mollie! Mollie! Bring that blue bottle!" cried Mummy anxiously.

Mollie heard her and scurried round faster and faster than ever after the buzzing bluebottle.

Upstairs, Baby's cough started getting worse.

"Mollie! Make haste!" cried Mummy. "Baby's not well!"

Mummy couldn't think why Mollie didn't come and she dared not wait any longer for Baby's medicine, so downstairs she went, holding Baby as gently as she could in her arms.

At the door she was met by Mollie, holding something tightly in one of her hands.

"I've got it, Mummy, I've got it!" she panted. "But it took me ever such a long time before I could catch it!"

"Catch it!" said Mummy. "Catch what? Whoever heard of any one catching medicine? Did the bottle walk right off the table and start to run round the room? Silly child! Look, there's the blue bottle of medicine I told you to get for baby, lying in the middle of the the table!"

Mollie stared at the medicine bottle.

"Oh!" she said, "I thought you meant this bluebottle fly I've caught," and she showed Mummy the little fly which she was holding in her hand.

"Ugh! The nasty thing! Throw it away and go and wash your

hands at once!" said Mummy, giving Baby his medicine. "You might have known I wouldn't have wanted anything like that for Baby, and if only you had listened to me and thought for a minute, you wouldn't have been so silly!"

"Oh dear! And I spent such a long time running round the room trying to catch that bluebottle fly," Mollie said. "I am a silly-billy, aren't I, Mummy?"

"You certainly are," said Mummy. "You are a real silly-billy. But you needn't be because you can think hard enough when you want to, Mollie, my dear!"

Mollie went very red.

"Please, is Baby all right now?" she asked.

"I think so," said Mummy, "but you know, Mollie, your thoughtlessness when you went to get the bottle might have been very serious for him and made him much worse. Go and wash your hands now."

Mollie went – and as she washed her hands she made her mind up to NEVER be so silly again, just in case she might go and hurt someone else by not thinking.

And what do you think

Mummy called her whenever she thought Mollie wasn't thinking enough? Miss Bluebottle!

The Vanishing
Nuts

IN the garden belonging to Apple Tree Cottage there were twenty-two nut trees. Susan, George and Peter's great-grandfather had planted them, because he had been very fond of nuts – and now they had grown into fine trees that bore heaps of big nuts every year.

Susan, George and Peter were very fond of nuts too. They helped to pick them and in return they were given a big dishful for themselves. They helped to pack up boxes of nuts too, to send away to Daddy's brother and sisters. Nut-time was a very busy time indeed!

Daddy always used to put aside a boxful of the very finest nuts for Christmas time. He carried it up into the attic room, and popped it on the floor there. Then, at Christmas, the box was taken downstairs and the nuts were set out in pretty little dishes.

One autumn the nut trees grew the biggest nuts they had had for years. Daddy was very pleased. He chose some fine ones to store away for Christmas, and George helped him to carry the box upstairs to the attic.

"Now, none of you children are to go to the attic for nuts," said

Daddy. "But you all know that, very well, don't you?"

"Yes, Daddy," said Susan, George and Peter. "We promise we won't."

Daddy didn't think any more about the Christmas nuts until one day when he happened to go upstairs to fetch a pair of old boots from the attic. He happened to glance at the box of nuts – and then he stood still and frowned.

"Someone's been taking those nuts," he said. "Now, whoever can it be?"

He went downstairs and found Mummy.

"Have you had to go up to the attic and take any of the Christmas nuts?" he asked.

"No, dear," said Mummy in surprise. "Why?"

"Because quite a number have gone," said Daddy, frowning. "Is it the children, do you think?"

"Oh, I hope not," said Mummy, looking worried. "I don't think they'd take anything without asking, do you?"

"Call them in here and I'll ask them," said Daddy. So Mummy called all of the children, who were out in the garden and the three of them soon came in and trooped into Daddy's study.

"Have any of you been taking the nuts from the attic?" said Daddy. "Have you, Susan?"

"Oh, no," said Susan. "Of course not, Daddy."

"What about you, George?" asked Daddy.

"I haven't either," said George.

"Have you, Peter?" said Daddy.

"No, I haven't," answered Peter. "Why, Daddy? Have the nuts gone?"

"A good many of them have," said Daddy. "Well, you may go. Remember never to take anything without asking, won't you?"

"Oh, yes, Daddy," said all the children, and off they went. But they were very worried, because they couldn't bear to think that Daddy should even dream that they could take the nuts without asking him first.

"Whoever can it be?" said Peter. "The baby-sitter hates nuts, so it can't be her."

"And the cleaning lady's been away ill for a month, so it can't be her!" said George.

"Well, that only leaves us three and Mummy and Daddy!" said Susan, puzzled. "Who on earth can it be?"

"We'll just wait and see if any

more go," said Peter. "Then, if they do, we'll have to do something about it!"

The next week, Daddy went up to the attic again, to look at the nuts – and dear me, a whole lot more had vanished! How puzzled and grieved he was! He felt certain that it must be one of the children.

But each of them said "No, Daddy," when he asked them.

"Well, it must be one of you," said Daddy, sadly. "It can't be anyone else. It grieves me very much, children, for I didn't think any of you would do such a stupid thing."

Susan went out of the room crying, for she loved her Daddy. George and Peter went very red, and when they were in the playroom they put their arms round Susan and hugged her and told her not to mind.

"It's not us, we know that," said George. "But it looks as if it quite easily might be us, so we can't blame Daddy for asking. The thing to do is to show him that it isn't us. Let's ask him to lock the door."

So they went to ask Daddy.

"Very well," he aside, and he locked the door and put the key in his pocket.

But still the nuts vanished! Daddy became more puzzled than ever. He simply couldn't make it out.

"Anyway, that proves it isn't us," said George, and Daddy smiled and said yes, it did, and he was very pleased indeed.

"I think it must be the fairies," said Susan. "Daddy, will you let us hide in the attic cupboard and watch one night?"

"No," said Daddy, laughing. "If you want to do any watching, you must do it in the day-time."

"But the fairies wouldn't come then." said Susan. But Daddy wouldn't agree to night-time watching, so Susan decided to watch in the day-time.

That afternoon the three children climbed the stairs to the attic, feeling rather excited. They were quite determined to catch the thief.

They went to the cupboard and settled themselves behind the curtains. For a long time nothing happened. Susan began to feel sleepy – but suddenly George poked her in the back.

"Sh! Sh!" he said. "Do you hear something?"

Susan and Peter listened. Yes! there was a little scrapy noise that was coming from somewhere. Then there was a bump and a slither, and a patter across the floor!

Was it the fairies? How the children's hearts beat! They peeped through the curtains, and watched the box of nuts. And then they saw the thief!

Who do you think it was? Why, it was the little grey squirrel who lived in the pine woods nearby! The pretty creature had climbed up a tree by the attic window, jumped to the top of the open window, leapt down, and come to the store of nuts every day!

"Oh!" said Susan, "so *that's* the thief! The pretty little fellow!"

The squirrel heard the children in the cupboard, and pricked up his ears. Suddenly George rushed out from behind the curtains and shut the window with a bang. The door was already shut, so the squirrel was fairly caught!

"Let's fetch Daddy!" said Susan. "Then he'll see who the thief is!"

So George opened the door a little way, and shouted "Daddy! Mummy!" Do come up to the attic! We've caught the thief!"

Daddy and Mummy came running up and slipped in through the door.

"There!" said Susan, pointing to the squirrel. "What do you think of our thief, Daddy?"

"Well, well, well!" said Daddy, in the greatest astonishment. "The little squirrel! Whoever would have thought it! He must have discovered our nuts and thought what a fine treasure-store he had found! Open the window and let him go, Peter."

The squirrel hopped out and disappeared down the tree.

"The mystery is solved," said Mummy, "and a good thing too! Come along downstairs, children, and I will give you a fine cherry cake for tea as a reward for your discovery!"

"Hurrah!" shouted the children, and off they rushed downstairs!

The
Buttercup
Spell

DO you know the story of the Buttercup Spell? Well, let me tell it to you.

It happened that a farmer many, many years ago, had a wonderful cow called Buttercup. Buttercup gave beautiful, creamy milk and from it the farmer's wife made the finest, golden butter in all the kingdom. Even the King and Queen sent a servant each day to buy some of the delicious butter to eat with their bread.

And then one day the farmer's wife found that there was a thief who was creeping into her dairy each night and stealing some of

the big, golden pats of butter!
But no one had seen the thief.
Who on earth could it be?

"Is it Diana, the dairymaid?"
she wondered. "No, she's an
honest girl. Is it Dan the
cowman? No, he has a cow of his
own and so he can have butter
whenever he likes. Is it Johnnie
who looks after the horses? No,
he never even comes near the
dairy. It can't be Jill the goose
girl either, because everyone
knows she never eats butter!"

But still, night by night, the
butter kept disappearing and yet
no dog ever barked when the
thief came.

"It must be someone the dogs know!" said the farmer. "We'll keep watch."

But though they kept watch every night, still the butter went. No one came in at the door. No one crept in at a window. Then who took the butter?

The farmer's wife went to her great-grandmother, who was a witch, and told her the whole story. The old dame listened and nodded her head.

"Ah – it must certainly be someone that loves butter and craves for it!" she said. "Someone who is very clever – clever enough to take it each

144

night under your very noses! Now, which cow did you say gives the milk that makes your finest butter?"

"Buttercup," said the farmer's wife. "And she's well-named, for her creamy milk makes the butter that is sent up to the royal palace every day!"

"Ah, Buttercup!" said the old dame. "Well, then, you must go out to the field and pick me the finest buttercup there that you can see. Bring it back to me and I will walk to your farm with you and then I will soon be able to find the thief who keeps stealing your butter!"

The farmer's wife picked a fine golden buttercup, whose cup shone just as if it had been freshly polished. The old witch walked back to the farm with her, and when they got there she spoke to the farmer.

"Call all your workers here, every one of them!"

One by one they came and stood round the old dame in surprise.

"Don't be afraid," she said. "I'm only using a simple buttercup spell, and that never did anyone any harm! Step forward, Diana the dairymaid."

Diana stood in front of the old

grand dame, half afraid. She knew the old woman was a witch. What kind of spell was she using? A buttercup spell? She had certainly never heard of a spell like that before.

The old woman took the buttercup and held it under the dairymaid's chin for a moment. Then she shook her head and pushed the girl away.

"She's not the one we want," she said. "Come forward, Johnnie the horse man."

Johnnie stepped forward, feeling very puzzled.

The old woman held the buttercup under his chin, peering

there as she did so. She shook her head again. "He's not the one," she said.

One by one all the farm workers came up to the old dame and held up their chins for her to hold the buttercup there. But each time she shook her head.

"It's none of these," she said. "Is this all? Are there no more workers on your farm?"

"Well, there's only Jill the goose girl," said the farmer's wife. "And she's out on the common with her geese. She never eats butter, so she can't be the thief."

"Fetch her," commanded the

old woman. "I must try every single one who works here with the spell."

The other workers went back to their tasks and the goose girl was sent for. She came with her geese behind her, a ragged little thing with big, frightened eyes.

"Here, lass, come and stand by me," commanded the old woman. "Do you like butter?"

"Yes, I like it very much. But I never eat it," said the goose girl in a scared voice. "I give my share to my mother. She's been ill for a long time."

"Stand still while I hold this buttercup under your chin," said

the old woman, and the goose
girl lifted her chin and stood
there, trembling.

The old dame held the
buttercup under the girl's chin –
and everyone saw a bright
golden glow there, that shone
like a small sun.

"Here is the thief," said the old
woman. "Jill the goose girl, who
says she never eats butter. She
must be punished, for she is
certainly wicked."

"I'm not, I'm not," wept the
girl. "As I said, I do like butter
very much, but I tell my mother
that I don't, so that she may have
my share. But she has been so ill

lately that I have had to steal a big pat of it for her each night. She needs butter and milk and eggs so badly, Mistress, to help her get better!"

"But however did you steal it?" asked the farmer's wife, who was feeling terribly sorry for the trembling girl.

"Mistress, I crept up on to the roof every night, and let down a basket through the skylight," wept the poor goose girl. "I put a long stick down and knocked a pat of butter into the basket and then drew it up again. The dogs didn't bark because, you see, they knew me."

"Poor child," said the farmer's wife kindly. "You did wrong, but I see how much you love your mother. Promise never to steal again and your mother shall have all the butter and milk and eggs that she needs."

"My buttercup spell found her out!" said the old witch. "And it will always find out those people who love butter and long to have it! That spell will last for a thousand years!"

She was right, wasn't she? Hold a buttercup under anyone's chin and see the spell still at work: anyone who loves butter will at once show a bright golden glow there, like a little sun, shining and gleaming! Have you ever tried it? What a strange bit of old, old magic!

A Story for Easter Time

THERE was once a chocolate shop in Fairyland, kept by old Mother Bootle. It was a most exciting shop. It had great big bottles full of sweets of all colours, wonderful boxes of chocolates, and candy, wrapped up in colourful paper.

But it was at Easter time that the shop was most colourful of all, for then Mother Bootle had so many Easter eggs she didn't know what to do.

And such GLORIOUS ones they were! Chocolate ones, marzipan ones that broke themselves in half when you said "Open Egg!" and showed you a surprise inside – perhaps a toy or a brooch. You can guess how all the fairies loved her shop.

One Easter her shop was fuller of eggs than ever before, and all day fairies, brownies, gnomes, and pixies looked in at the window longingly. They looked especially at one great big egg tied up with gold ribbon right in the very middle of the window. It was a magic egg, and very expensive indeed.

Now Oll, the gnome, longed to buy that egg. So he counted out his gold, and he found he had twenty pieces. He tied them up in a bag and sat down to think.

"I don't believe that egg's worth more than twenty pieces of gold," he said, "but perhaps Mother Bootle wouldn't let me have it for that. The best thing to do would be to go into her shop when she is having her dinner, leave the money on the counter and take the egg."

So you can see by that, that he was not a very nice little gnome. He ran off to the shop. It was just dinner time. He peeped inside. No one was there. Mother Bootle was having her dinner.

Quickly, Oll slipped inside, put his money-bag on the counter, caught up the magic egg, and ran! The egg was very heavy, for it was half as big as Oll himself.

He panted and puffed all the way home, and when he got there he put the egg down on his table and looked at it proudly.

"I'll untie the ribbon and say, 'Open Egg!'" he said, "and see what happens! I might find all sorts of wonderful things inside!"

He untied the gold ribbon.

"Open Egg!" he cried in a loud voice.

In a trice the egg flew open, and out jumped a little imp! Oll looked just as scared as could be. He had never thought of anything like that at all.

"What can I do for you?" asked the imp, grinning. "I am your servant."

"Dear me, is that so?" said Oll, beginning to feel better. "Well, well! Let me see! You can sweep my bedroom for me!"

The imp took a broom, leapt upstairs, and began sweeping.

Oll heard him – swish! swish! swish!

"Well, that's very nice," said Oll. "Now I've got a servant who will do all my work!"

He settled himself in a cosy chair and began to read.

Swish! Swish! Swish! went the broom upstairs. Swish! Swish!

"He's doing it very thoroughly!" said Oll after a time, "I'd better go and see if he's finished."

He ran upstairs, but oh, my goodness! That imp had swept the bedroom nearly bare! He had swept up chairs and pictures, stools and books, and now he was beginning to sweep them out of the window.

"Stop!" cried Oll. "Stop! Whatever are you doing?"

"I can't stop working until you say the proper words!" said the imp, sweeping a chair out of the window. "I'm magic!"

Well, Oll tried all the words he

knew, but nothing he could think of stopped that imp.

"Perhaps you'd better tell me to do some other sort of work!" said the imp at last, when he had swept nearly everything out of the window or down the stairs. "I can do any work you like, you know!"

"Dear, dear, I wish I'd known that before," said Oll. "Go into the garden and wash my dirty dusters, then."

At once the imp ran downstairs, took a tub and water, and began to wash Oll's dirty dusters, whilst the gnome tried to put his bedroom straight.

Suddenly he heard shouts of laughter coming from the road outside, and looking out of the window, he saw a crowd of fairies and pixies leaning over his garden wall and laughing.

It must be something that imp was doing! Oll rushed downstairs and out into the garden.

The imp had washed all the dusters and pegged them on the line, but he couldn't stop washing till he was told do something else. So what do you think he had done?

He rushed indoors and fetched the tables and chairs, and washed those! Then he had hung them on the line, and you can't think how silly they all looked! It was no wonder everyone was laughing. He was just going to peg up a lot of saucepans when Oll rushed out.

"Stop! Stop!" he cried.

"I can't!" said the imp, grinning. "I'm magic! Think of something else for me to do!"

Well, will you believe it? Oll couldn't think of a single thing to tell the imp to do next! He just stood there, trying his hardest to think of something.

And then a dreadful thing happened.

The imp thought he would

wash Oll next, and so he suddenly grabbed hold of him, put him in the tub and soaped him all over!

"Splutter! Splutter! Splish-splash! Splutter!" went Oll, with soap in his mouth, eyes and nose. "Help! Help! Fetch Mother Bootle, quick, somebody! Fetch Mother Bootle!"

One of the watching fairies flew off, laughing, to fetch Mother Bootle. Poor Oll had the water squeezed out of him, and then the wicked imp began to peg him on the line to dry!

And that's where Mother Bootle found him when she came

hurrying down the road! She laughed till the tears ran down her cheeks to see Oll among all the chairs and saucepans!

"I took your magic egg!" wept Oll, "but I'm sorry. Tell your imp to stop! I don't know how to make him!"

"Easy enough!" said Mother Bootle. "Go back to your egg!" she said to the imp.

Bang! Clap! He was gone, and through the open door Oll saw the split egg close together again.

Mother Bootle unpegged him from the line.

"Well, you've been well punished for your dishonesty,

Oll," she said. "You can have your gold back, unless you want to keep the egg. Do you?"

"No, no, no!" cried Oll. "Take the magic egg away. That imp has turned my house upside down, and made everyone laugh at me! Take the egg away!"

So Mother Bootle took the egg home, and left Oll to make his house tidy again. The egg was never seen in the window any more, and what happened to it nobody knows. But people do say it will turn up again one day.

I'm sure I don't want it, though, do you?

The Bright
Little Pound

MARY and John had such a nice surprise one morning. Mother told them that Uncle Jack had been to see her the night before, when they were in bed – and had left a bright new pound coin for the two children!

How pleased they were!

"Oh, Mother, Ronald and Joan are coming to tea today!" said Mary. "Can we spend the money on some cakes? You said you wouldn't have time to make any for us today."

"You can spend it how you like," said Mother, smiling. "The baker should be coming soon. You can go and keep a good look out for him."

So Mary and John ran out of doors and swung on the gate, looking for the baker's cart. They knew it quite well. It was not very big, and a pony pulled it. They often heard his hooves going clip-clop-clip-clop down the road.

"Look!" said John. "There's the mail van outside the post office! I expect there are a lot of parcels and letters today!"

As he spoke, a postman came out with two large sacks. He threw them into the red mail van and then went back for some more. Another postman came

out of the post office with a sack
– but he did not go to the mail
van, he walked down the street.
He had some letters to deliver to
people's houses!

Soon the children heard rat-a-
tat-tat all the way down the road.
It was fun watching the postman
going to the different houses.
Once he had to stop until the
door was opened, because there
was a parcel to hand in.

"Here's the baker's cart!" said
Mary at last. "I can hear the
pony going clip-clop! Hurrah!
Now we can choose our cakes!

Don't let's wait till the baker
gets here, John. Let's go and buy

them right now!"

The children scampered down the road to the baker. He had opened his cart at the back, and was taking out a basket.

"Baker, Baker, have you any nice cakes today?" asked Mary, running up. "We have some money to spend, and we want to buy some cakes for tea."

"I have some nice currant buns," said the baker. He took out a tray of cakes and buns and showed them to the children.

"Oh, we'll have two buns, please," said John. "I love buns. They look nice, sticky ones, too!"

"That's twenty pence," said the

baker "Is there anything else you would like?"

"How much are these sugary cakes?" asked Mary, pointing to some iced cakes with jam in them. "They look lovely."

"They are four for fifty-five pence," said the baker. "There are some pink ones and some white ones. Would you like two pink and two white?"

"Oh yes" said John. So the baker put the two buns and the four iced cakes into a bag and gave it to the children. How pleased they were! They gave him their pound coin.

"There's twenty-five pence

change, said the baker. "Twenty pence for the buns, and fifty-five pence for the cakes – twenty and fifty-five make seventy-five. Twenty-five pence change!"

The children said thank you, and ran home with their cakes.

"What shall we do with the twenty-five pence?" asked Mary.

"I know!' said John. We shall write a postcard to thank Uncle Jack for the pound and we will buy a stamp with the last twenty five pence!"

"Good idea!" said Mary. "I'll get one of my postcards now."

So she got one that she had painted herself, and together the

children made up what to write.
"Dear Uncle Jack, Thank you
for your nice new pound coin.
We have bought two buns and
four cakes with it, and we are
buying a stamp for this postcard.
Love from Mary and John!"

Mother said it was written very
nicely. She said they might go to
the post office and buy a stamp
and post the card themselves. So
off they went.

"I'll buy the stamp and you can
post the card," said John. So they
went into the big post office, and
pushed their money over the
counter. The girl gave them a
first-class stamp. John stuck it on

the card. They went out and Mary ran to the letter box. She posted the card and both children heard it go plop! It was safely in the box! The postman would take it out and another postman would deliver it to Uncle Jack.

"What fun we've had with that pound coin!" said Mary. "Two buns, four cakes and a first-class stamp! The baker and the postman have worked hard for us today. What would we do without them!"

The Runaway Hat

IT all happened because the wind blew Jim's hat off. It blew so hard that the elastic snapped, and away went the straw hat, bowling over and over as it rolled down the hill.

"Run after it, Jim!" said Auntie Kate. "Quickly, or it will be lost!"

Jim ran after it, and soon got up to the rolling hat. For a moment it lay still, but just as Jim stooped to pick it up, the wind gave a puff, and sent the hat on again.

What was more annoying still, Jim felt absolutely certain he heard a low, chuckling laugh, right by his ear.

He looked round. No, nobody was near! Who had laughed, then? Surely it couldn't have been the wind!

He ran on again after his hat. It was bowling on, far in front of him, jumping over puddles as if it knew it mustn't go into them.

Then it lay still again.

"Ha!" said Jim. "I'll get you this time!"

He raced on as fast as he could. He bent down to his hat and caught hold of the brim – but, "Well, I'm bothered!" said Jim – for the wind jerked it out of his hand and sent it flying into the wood at the side of the road.

And by his ear came that gurgling chuckle again! Just as if somebody were laughing till the tears ran down his cheeks.

Jim looked all round. No one was near.

"All right," said Jim. "I can hear you, Mr Wind! I think it's jolly mean of you to take away my hat, but I'm going to catch it, so there!"

He ran into the wood and looked about for his hat. Yes, there it was, caught in a branch of a tree.

"I can easily climb that!" said Jim, and looked for a place that would be easy to get up.

But would you believe it? No sooner was he climbing up than the wind blew the hat off the branch and sent it down on the ground again. It really was most tiresome.

Jim climbed down. The hat lay away in the distance, half buried in last year's leaves. Jim decided to stalk it, as a cat stalks a bird.

"I believe the hat is helping the wind to tease me!" he thought.

So he dodged from tree to tree until he had nearly reached the heap of dead leaves where he thought the hat lay.

Then suddenly out he pounced

and caught hold of it.

But it wasn't the hat! It was a great white toadstool that broke in his hands! Jim heard the wind laugh again, and saw the hat running away in front of him

Jim was growing cross. On he went again, determined not to stop running until he caught that hat. He was quickly catching it up. He would soon have it – two or three steps more – a grab – and, oh!

The hat had rolled right into a little pond that lay hidden in a dip in the wood. There it floated, upside down, green with weed and brown with mud.

"Very well," said Jim. "You're a very silly hat. I shall leave you there alone. I'm sure I don't want to wear you any more!"

He thought he heard a laugh behind him. Yes, there it was again, farther off, beyond the nearby trees.

"I'll go and catch that rascally wind if I can!" thought Jim, and immediately set off in the direction of the laugh.

Now and again he heard the chuckling and each time he ran in the direction it came from. After a while he stood still. He could hear no laughing. The wind was gone.

But hark! What was that contented humming sound? Jim listened. Then he stole towards the hazel trees in front of him, and peeped round them.

What he saw made him stare as if he could not believe his eyes.

He saw a beautiful little glade, full of wild, white anemones, each with her dainty little frills of green. And they were dancing, every one of them – nodding and swaying, shaking out their little green frills and looking as pretty as a picture.

And kneeling down among them was the wind! He was blowing here and blowing there, making the flowers dance for him in every corner.

Jim watched for a minute. Then he said:

"Mr Wind! Do you know what you have done to my hat?"

The wind turned round in surprise.

"Hello! Why, it's Jim!" He smiled. "Yes, I blew your hat off for a joke!"

"Well, it's rolled into the pond, and I can't wear it any more," said Jim. "I think it's very unkind of you."

"Oh dear! Oh dear!" said the wind. "I didn't mean to do that! I must have blown too hard! I'm really very sorry."

"I don't mind a joke," said Jim. "I think jokes are funny, even when they're played on me – but to lose my hat altogether isn't a joke, I can tell you."

"Well, I'd give you my hat to make up for it," said the wind, looking very worried, "only I haven't got one. My brother, the North Wind, blew it away the other day. Would you accept a few of my flowers instead? They're the only ones out, you know, and this is my special garden."

"They are certainly out very early," said Jim. "Yes, I'd like some, please. They'll make up for losing my hat."

The wind picked him a lovely bunch of the dainty little anemones, told him the quickest way out of the wood, laughed, and vanished.

Jim went back up the hill to his Auntie and showed her his bunch of flowers.

"Good gracious, Jim!" she cried. "Wherever did you find those flowers? I've never seen them out so early in the year before! How perfectly lovely!"

"The wind sent my hat into a pond," said Jim, "and gave me these flowers to make up for it.

Do you know what they are called, Auntie Kate?"

"They're anemones," said Auntie Kate, "But people call them windflowers, because they dance so prettily in the wind."

"So that's why he's got his garden full of them!" said Jim to himself. "They're his very own flowers! No wonder they dance so prettily when he blows."

And I think when you see the windflowers nodding and swaying whenever the south wind blows, you will say too that there couldn't be a better name for the little dancing flowers of the spring.